MATH ADVENTURES

BRADY BAKES A CAKE

A MEASURING ADVENTURE

by Megan Atwood
illustrated by Amy Zhing

GRASSHOPPER

Tools for Parents & Teachers

Grasshopper Books enhance imagination and introduce the earliest readers to fiction with fun storylines and illustrations. The easy-to-read text supports early reading experiences with repetitive sentence patterns and sight words.

Before Reading

- Look at the cover illustration. What do readers see? What do they think the book will be about?
- Look at the picture glossary together. Sound out the words. Ask readers to identify the first letter of each vocabulary word.

Read the Book

- "Walk" through the book, reading to or along with the reader. Point to the illustrations as you read.

After Reading

- Review the picture glossary again. Ask readers to locate the words in the text.
- Ask the reader: Brady bakes a birthday cake for his mom. Have you ever baked anything? Did you measure the ingredients?

Grasshopper Books are published by Jump!
5357 Penn Avenue South
Minneapolis, MN 55419
www.jumplibrary.com

Library of Congress Cataloging-in-Publication Data

Names: Atwood, Megan, author. | Zhing, Amy, illustrator.
Title: Brady bakes a cake: a measuring adventure
by Megan Atwood; illustrated by Amy Zhing.
Description: Minneapolis, MN: Jump!, Inc., [2022]
Series: Math adventures
Audience: Ages 4-7.
Identifiers: LCCN 2021038105 (print)
LCCN 2021038106 (ebook)
ISBN 9781636906263 (hardcover)
ISBN 9781636906270 (paperback)
ISBN 9781636906287 (ebook)
Subjects: LCSH: Readers (Primary)
Measurement–Juvenile fiction.
LCGFT: Readers (Publications)
Classification: LCC PE1119.2.A8928 2022 (print)
LCC PE1119.2 (ebook) | DDC 428.6/2–dc23
LC record available at https://lccn.loc.gov/2021038105
LC ebook record available at https://lccn.loc.gov/2021038106

Editor: Eliza Leahy
Direction and Layout: Anna Peterson
Illustrator: Amy Zhing

Printed in the United States of America at
Corporate Graphics in North Mankato, Minnesota.

Table of Contents

Measure and Mix

"Let's bake a cake!" says Brady.

He reads the recipe.

He has all the ingredients.

He adds butter to a bowl.

Now he needs 1 cup of sugar.

But he can only find a ½ cup to measure with.

"I know!" he says.

He measures two ½ cups.

½ CUP + ½ CUP = 1 CUP
SUGAR

He adds the eggs and milk.

Now he needs 1½ teaspoons of vanilla.

He only has a ½ teaspoon.

Brady knows what to do!

$\frac{1}{2} + \frac{1}{2} + \frac{1}{2} = 1\frac{1}{2}$
MILK

Next is flour.

He needs $1\frac{1}{2}$ cups.

Brady adds 1 cup.

Then he adds two $\frac{1}{4}$ cups!

1 + 1/4 + 1/4 = 1 1/2
FLOUR

His dad helps mix the ingredients.

The cake bakes.

Then Brady frosts it.

Yum!

The cake is ready!

"Happy birthday, Mom!" Brady says.

Let's Review!

Brady measured ingredients to bake a cake. How many ¼ cups are in 1 cup?

A. 1 **B.** 2 **C.** 3 **D.** 4

Picture Glossary

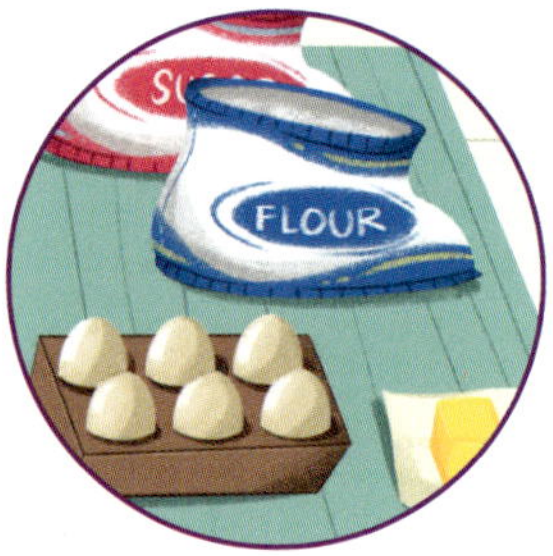

ingredients
Items used to make something.

measure
To portion out the amount of something.

recipe
Instructions for preparing food.

teaspoon
A small spoon used to measure in cooking.

Let's Review! Answer Key: **D.** 4